PRAYERS
FOR CHILDREN

Pictures by Eloise Wilkin

A GOLDEN BOOK • NEW YORK
Western Publishing Company, Inc., Racine, Wisconsin 53404

A Time-Tested Golden Book

Acknowledgments

"A Great Gray Elephant" is reprinted by the permission of The National Society for the Prevention of Blindness, Inc.

Dear Father,
Hear and Bless

Dear Father,
   hear and bless
Thy beasts
   and singing birds:
And guard
   with tenderness
Small things
   that have no words.

Morning Prayer

Now, before I run to play,
  Let me not forget to pray
To God Who kept me through the night
  And waked me with the morning light.

Help me, Lord, to love Thee more
  Than I ever loved before,
In my work and in my play,
  Be Thou with me through the day.

                              Amen.

I Thank Thee, Lord

I thank Thee, Lord, for quiet rest,
And for Thy care of me;
O let me through this day be blest
And kept from harm by Thee.
— Mary L. Duncan

Father, We Thank Thee

For flowers that bloom about our feet,
    Father, we thank Thee,
For tender grass so fresh and sweet,
    Father, we thank Thee,
For the song of bird and hum of bee,
For all things fair we hear or see
Father in heaven, we thank Thee.

For blue of stream and blue of sky,
    Father, we thank Thee,
For pleasant shade of branches high,
    Father, we thank Thee,
For fragrant air and cooling breeze,
For beauty of the blooming trees,
Father in heaven, we thank Thee.

For this new morning with its light,
    Father, we thank Thee,
For rest and shelter of the night,
    Father, we thank Thee,
For health and food, for love and friends,
For everything Thy goodness sends,
Father in heaven, we thank Thee.

— Ralph Waldo Emerson

A Great Gray Elephant

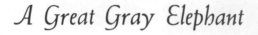

great gray elephant,
A little yellow bee,
A tiny purple violet,
A tall green tree,
A red and white sailboat
On a blue sea—
All these things
You gave to me,
When you made
My eyes to see—
Thank you, God!

Be Present at Our Table, Lord

Be present at our table, Lord,
Be here and everywhere adored.
These morsels bless, and grant that we
May feast in Paradise with Thee. Amen.

The Lord's Prayer

ur Father, Who art in heaven,
Hallowed be Thy Name.
Thy kingdom come,
Thy will be done,
In earth as it is in heaven.
Give us this day our daily bread,
And forgive us our debts,
As we forgive our debtors.
And lead us not into temptation
But deliver us from evil,
For thine is the kingdom,
And the power, and the glory,
Forever. Amen.

The Doxology

Praise God, from whom all blessings flow;
Praise Him, all creatures here below;
Praise Him above, ye heavenly host:
Praise Father, Son, and Holy Ghost. Amen.

Jesus, from Thy Throne on High

Jesus, from Thy throne on high,
   Far above the bright blue sky,
Look on me with loving eye;
   Hear me, Holy Jesus.

Be Thou with me every day,
   In my work and in my play,
When I learn and when I pray;
   Hear me, Holy Jesus.

— Thomas B. Pollock

The Gift

What can I give Him,
   Poor as I am?
If I were shepherd
   I would bring a lamb,
If I were a Wise Man
   I would do my part,—
Yet what can I give Him,
   Give my heart.

          — Christina Rossetti

Good-Night Prayer

Father, unto Thee I pray,
Thou hast guarded me all day;
Safe I am while in Thy sight,
Safely let me sleep tonight.

Bless my friends, the whole world bless;
Help me to learn helpfulness;
Keep me ever in Thy sight;
So to all I say good night.

— Henry Johnstone

Bedtime Prayer

Now I lay me down to sleep,
I pray Thee, Lord, thy child to keep:
Thy love guard me through the night
And wake me with the morning light.
                              Amen.

Good Night

Good night! Good night! Far flies the light;
But still God's love shall flame above,
Making all bright. Good night! Good night!

God Watches Us

God watches o'er us all the day, at home, at school, and at our play;
And when the sun has left the skies, he watches with a million eyes.
— Gabriel Setoun

Evening Prayer

Words adapted by Miriam Drury

Miriam Drury

Now I lay me down to sleep, I pray Thee, Lord, Thy child to keep: Thy love guard me through the night, And wake me with the morn-ing light.

BIBLE
PICTURE STORIES

BIBLE
PICTURE STORIES
From the Old and New Testaments

As told by Carol Mullan

Illustrated by Gordon Laite

A GOLDEN BOOK • NEW YORK
Western Publishing Company, Inc., Racine, Wisconsin 53404

Soon it will rain so hard that the whole world will be covered with water. Noah and his family and all the animals will be safe in this boat called an ark.

Gen. 7:13-23

Jacob has made a fine coat of many colors to give to his son Joseph. Joseph knows that his father loves him very much.

Gen. 37:3

Joseph has been in Egypt for many years. He is very happy to see his younger brother, Benjamin, and his ten older brothers again. They are glad to see him, too.

Gen. 43-45

Pharaoh's daughter has found baby Moses' basket.
When she opens it, he cries. She feels sorry for the
baby and decides to take care of him. Moses' sister,
Miriam, watches nearby and is glad.

Exod. 2:1-10

When Moses holds his rod over the sea, God makes a wide, dry path so that Moses' people can get to the other side. The wicked Pharaoh and his soldiers will not catch them now.

Exod. 14:5-29

God gave Moses many laws to help the people to live better. Moses carries some of the laws, written on two stone tablets, down from Mount Sinai. We call these laws the Ten Commandments.

Exod. 31:18; 32:15-16; 34:1-4, 27-28

Naomi and Ruth have come to Bethlehem to live. Ruth gathers corn and barley in the fields of Boaz so that she and Naomi will have something to eat. Boaz tells his men to leave many sheaves of barley for her.

Ruth 1:11-2:18

God has told Samuel the prophet to choose a new king to rule over Israel. Samuel sends for Jesse's youngest son, David the shepherd boy. He will be the new king.

1 Sam. 16:1-12

Commanded by God, ravens bring bread and meat to Elijah. He gets water to drink from the brook that runs near the cave where he is hiding.

1 Kings 17:1-6

The beautiful and good Queen Esther goes to see the king. She wants to persuade him to save her people, the Jews, from the evil Haman. The king loves his wife, and he listens to her. The Jews will be safe.

Esther 2:16-7:10

Lying in a manger, baby Jesus looks up at the shepherds who have come to Bethlehem to see him. Mary, his mother, and Joseph, her husband, smile at Jesus.

Luke 2:15-16

Jesus listens to the men in the temple. Although he is only twelve years old, he knows he must learn many things. The men are surprised at how well he understands what they say.

Luke 2:41-47

Peter's mother-in-law is one of the sick people whom Jesus heals. As he takes her hand and helps her up, her fever goes away, and she is well again.

Matt. 8:14-17; Mark 1:29-34; Luke 4:38-40

A little boy shares his dinner with the people who came
to listen to Jesus. Jesus blesses the five little loaves of
bread and the two small fish, and then his twelve disciples pass them out to the people. Everyone has all he
wants to eat.

Matt. 14:14-21; Mark 6:34-44; Luke 9:11-17; John 6:5-13

Jesus rides into Jerusalem on the back of a young ass.
He is going to the feast of the Passover. Many people
spread cloth and branches in his path and shout with
joy when they see him.

Matt. 21:1-9; Mark 11:1-10; Luke 19:29-38; John 12:12-15

Unaware that Jesus will soon be betrayed by Judas,
Peter, James, and John sleep peacefully. Not far away,
Jesus asks his heavenly Father to help him.

Matt. 26:36-46; Mark 14:32-42; Luke 22:39-47

Standing outside the tomb where he was buried, Jesus speaks to Mary Magdalene. How happy she is to see that he is alive again. Now he will live forever.

Mark 16:9; John 20:11-17; Rev. 1:18

BIBLE PICTURE STORIES

NEW TESTAMENT BIBLE STORIES

As told by Carol Mullan • Illustrated by Dan Waring

A GOLDEN BOOK • NEW YORK
Western Publishing Company, Inc., Racine, Wisconsin 53404

Elisabeth and Zacharias were sad. They had prayed many times for children. But they didn't have any, and now they were old. Then an angel came to Zacharias in the temple and told him that their prayers were answered. Elisabeth was going to have a baby, who was to be named John. John was going to be a very special prophet. He would help people to get ready for Jesus, the Savior.

Zacharias wanted to believe the angel, but when he thought about how old he and his wife were, he doubted the angel's words. Because he did not believe what the angel had said, he was no longer able to speak. Whenever he wanted to say anything, he had to write it down.

When the baby was born, the neighbors and relatives thought he should be named Zacharias, after his father. But Zacharias remembered what the angel had said, and he wrote that the baby's name was to be John. When Zacharias finished writing, he was able to talk again. He told the neighbors and relatives that John was going to be a special prophet. How excited they were to learn that the Savior was soon to come to them and that John would help them to get ready for him!

Jesus went from place to place, telling people how they must live while on earth, in order to please God and to live with him in heaven after they died. With power given to him by his heavenly Father, Jesus healed the sick people who came to him believing that he could help them.

Jesus knew that he wouldn't be on earth very long, so he chose twelve men to be his special helpers, called apostles. Putting his hands on the head of each apostle, Jesus gave each one the power to heal sick people in his name. He also prepared them to teach people, just as he did.

Sometimes the apostles did not understand very well. Once they asked Jesus which of his disciples, or followers, was the most important. Jesus called a little child to him and told the apostles that the one who was most important would be as obedient and trusting and loving as the little child in front of them.

Jesus knew that the apostles didn't understand, because another time, when little children were brought to Jesus to be blessed, the apostles tried to send them away. Jesus again explained how important little children are to God. Then Jesus took all of the children in his arms, one by one, and blessed them.

Jesus and his apostles often walked many, many miles over hot, dusty roads in order to teach people. When they finally stopped to eat and rest for the night, they were tired. Their feet were dirty because the roads were full of dust.

One night, after fastening a towel around himself, Jesus filled a basin with water and began to wash the apostles' feet. The apostles were astonished at first; they didn't know what to think. Then they felt ashamed to have Jesus wash their feet. He was the Savior of the world, and the Savior shouldn't be washing their feet, they thought.

Jesus told them not to be ashamed of doing anything to help people. Just as he was helping them, they should help each other.

People often came from far away to listen to Jesus. One day, when the people had listened many hours and it was almost night, Jesus knew that they must be hungry. He asked his apostles if anyone had brought anything to eat. Andrew told Jesus that there was a young boy who had five loaves of bread and two small fish. But that was not very much food to share with five thousand people.

While the apostles had the people sit in groups of fifty, the boy gladly gave his bread and fish to Jesus to share with the people. Jesus looked toward heaven and blessed the food, and as he divided it among the apostles, there was plenty. The apostles passed the food to all the people, and everyone ate until he was full.

Jesus loved to tell stories that helped people to understand what they must do to be better. One story helped them to understand that God loved them, even if they were bad, but that he was happiest when they stopped being bad and, by being good, came back to him.

The story Jesus told was about a man who had two sons. The younger son asked his father for the money he was supposed to get when he was older. He took the money and went to a faraway country, where he spent it all on parties and foolish things.

When his money was gone, the younger son had to work as a servant, feeding pigs. There was a famine in that faraway country, and the younger son never had enough to eat. He thought about how nice it had been to live at home with his father and his older brother.

Deciding he would rather be a servant for his father than starve where he was, the younger son went home to ask his father to forgive him and hire him as a servant. But when his father saw him coming, he ran eagerly to meet him. Then the father had a big dinner prepared to celebrate his younger son's return.

The older son didn't understand why his father was so happy to see the younger son. The father explained that he was happy because the younger son had stopped doing bad things and had come home to him.

Jesus warned people that just listening to his teachings would not get them to heaven. They would have to believe in him and do what he taught them to do if they were to live in heaven with God after they died.

If they obeyed him, he explained, they would be like the wise man who built his house upon a big rock. When the storm came, the wise man didn't have to worry, because his house was safe.

But the people who didn't obey him, Jesus went on, would be like the foolish man who built his house upon sand. When the storm came, his house fell apart.

Sometimes Jesus taught people by asking them questions.

One time he told them to pretend they had a hundred sheep. If one of the sheep were lost, he asked them, wouldn't they leave their other sheep in order to find the lost one? And when they found it, wouldn't they tell their friends and neighbors, so that the friends and neighbors could be happy about it, too?

Jesus wanted the people to understand that, just as the one lost sheep was important to them, each one of them was important to him. He loved each and every one of them.

A neighbor, Jesus explained, is not just someone who lives near you. A neighbor is someone who is happy when you are happy and sad when you are sad. A real neighbor helps you when you are in trouble. Everyone should be a good neighbor, Jesus said. To help people to understand what a good neighbor does, he told this story:

A Jew was going from Jerusalem to Jericho, when thieves beat him and robbed him and left him to die by the side of the road. A priest went by, and so did a Levite. Both men lived near the man, but neither stopped to help him.

Then a Samaritan saw him. Although the Jews and the Samaritans were enemies, this Samaritan bandaged the wounds of the Jew. Then, putting the wounded man on his own donkey, the Samaritan took him to an inn. The Samaritan even paid the innkeeper to take care of the man until he felt better.

Though he lived much farther from the Jew than did the priest or the Levite, the Samaritan was the real neighbor to him.

People knew that Jesus could heal those who were sick, but sometimes the crowds around him were so large that the sick people could not get close enough to ask his help.

One woman had been sick for twelve years. She had gone to many doctors, but no one could help her. When she saw Jesus, she squeezed through the crowd until she could reach out and touch his clothing.

Jesus felt some of his healing power leave him, and he turned around to see who had touched him. He told the woman that she was healed because she believed in him.

Because God was Jesus' father, Jesus had power over death. Three days after he had died, Jesus was resurrected — his spirit went back into his body, and he would never die again.

Even though Jesus had taught people about life after death, he knew that they didn't understand. Not even the apostles really understood, until Jesus went to see them after he was resurrected. Jesus talked with the apostles. He ate a piece of fish and some honey to show them that he truly was alive. And he told them to touch him, so they would know that what they heard and saw was real.

Jesus stayed with the apostles for a while, and then he went to heaven to live with his heavenly Father.

The apostles wanted to tell everyone about Jesus. They were glad when great crowds of people came from near and far for a feast called the Feast of Pentecost.

The apostles didn't know how to speak in all the different languages of the people who came for the feast. But, as the apostles started to tell the people about Jesus, each person who listened to them understood—in his own language—what the apostles were saying.

Many, many people became disciples of Jesus that day.

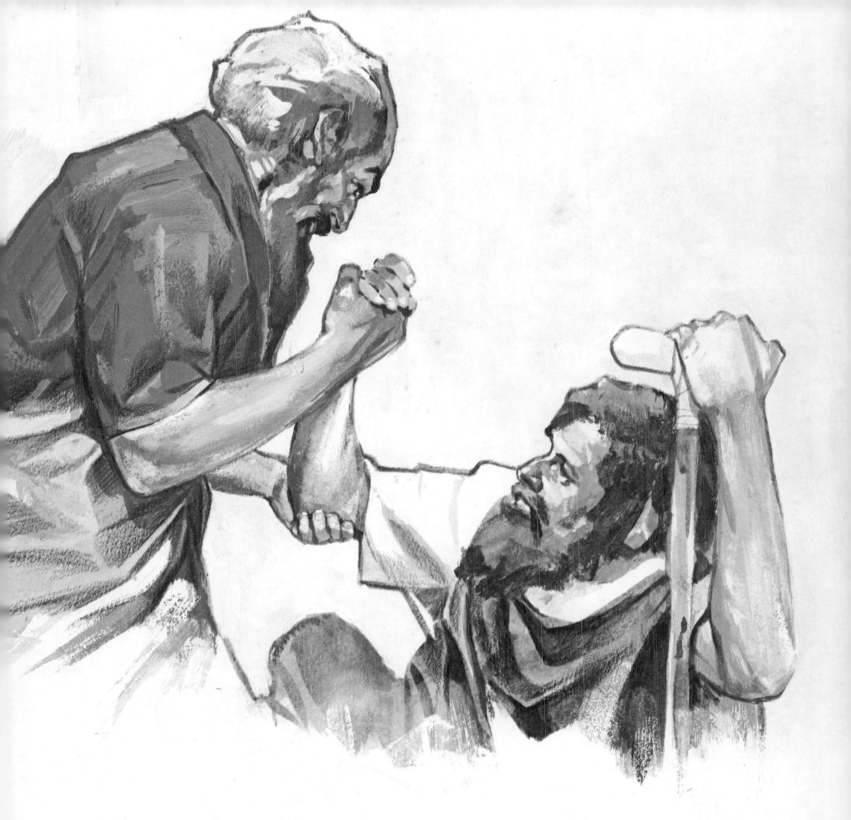

Peter and John, two of Jesus' apostles, went to the temple in Jerusalem to pray. As they came to the gate of the temple, they saw a man begging for money. The man had been crippled all his life and couldn't walk.

Peter didn't have any money, but he gave the beggar something better than money. Telling him that he was being healed in Jesus' name, Peter took the man by his right hand and helped him up.

The man was so happy to be healed that he ran and leaped about. Then he went into the temple with Peter and John to praise God.

From the time he was a little boy in Cilicia, Paul had obeyed the laws of Moses. He thought that Jesus and his disciples were teaching people to disobey the laws of Moses, so he tried to get them thrown into prison.

When Paul was going to Damascus with some other men, to find more of Jesus' disciples to put into prison, a very bright light suddenly shone all around him. The light was so bright that Paul was blinded, and he fell to the ground. Then he heard Jesus' voice asking him why he was hurting the disciples.

Once he understood that Jesus was the Savior that Moses had written about, Paul realized that he had been harming good people. Paul was sorry, and he wanted to know what he could do to help Jesus.

Jesus told him to go on to Damascus. The men who were with Paul led him to the house of a man named Judas. Three days later, Ananias, a disciple, came to him. Ananias told Paul that Jesus had sent him; then he put his hands on Paul's head and blessed him so that he could see again.

Paul was baptized right away. Then he went to Rome and Greece and many other places, to tell as many people as he could about Jesus.

Cornelius was an officer in the Roman army. He was a good man, and he was trusted by everyone who knew him. He and his family believed in Jesus, but they didn't know how to become Jesus' disciples.

An angel came to Cornelius as he was praying. The angel said that Cornelius should ask Peter to come and teach him how to become Jesus' disciple. Now, Peter had never taught anyone except Jews before, but an angel told him to go with the men Cornelius had sent.

Peter taught Cornelius and all his family. How glad Peter was to know that God wanted everyone to be disciples of Jesus!